The First Year: A Marble Grant Novel

Ghost Diet & Other Marble Grant Stories

Ashes to Weddings & Other Marble Grant Stories

A Big Twisted Plot & Other Marble Grant Stories

PAKHET JONES

The Big Tom: A Packet Jones Short Novel

Big Eyes: A Packet Jones Short Novel

THUNDER MOUNTAIN

Thunder Mountain

Monumental Summit

Avalanche Creek

The Edwards Mansion

Lake Roosevelt

Warm Springs

Melody Ridge

Grapevine Springs

The Idanha Hotel

The Taft Ranch

Tombstone Canyon

Dry Creek Crossing

Hot Springs Meadow

Green Valley

SEEDERS UNIVERSE

Dust and Kisses: A Seeders Universe Prequel Novel

Against Time

Sector Justice

Morning Song

The High Edge

Star Mist

Star Rain

Star Fall

Starburst

Rescue Two

COLD POKER GANG

Kill Game

Cold Call

Calling Dead

Bad Beat

Dead Hand

Freezeout

Ace High

Burn Card

Heads Up

Ring Game

Bottom Pair

THEY'RE BACK

Poker Boy Origin Novella

Dean Wesley Smith

CONTENTS

THEY'RE BACK

THEY'RE BACK

CHAPTER 1

NOT POSSIBLE, BUT FACT

"The Slots of Saturn are back," Stan, the God of Poker said to me as he slid into the booth beside Patty.

I laughed and pointed out the window. "Pig just flew by. Pink, a ribbon on its tail. Really flapping hard."

Patty giggled and shook her head.

Stan said nothing, didn't even laugh at my stupid joke.

"Wait, just saw another."

Again he didn't laugh or even shake his head in disgust, which he often did when I got really silly.

Both Patty and I just stared at him, waiting for his punch line. He had just said that the Slots of Saturn were back. That had to be a joke with a really stupid punch line, because those monsters were not a laughing matter.

But no punch line was coming, at least none that I could

tell. Trying to get a read on the God of Poker was just about impossible. He had the best poker face on the planet and with his tan slacks, button-down brown cardigan sweater and short brown hair, he could make himself invisible in a crowd without any powers at all.

"Sorry, Poker Boy, Patty," Stan said. "I can't believe it either."

"Serious?" I asked. "No flying pigs with pink ribbons?"

"Serious," he said.

Patty and I had been having a quiet lunch in my invisible office, floating high over the Las Vegas strip. I should have known a wonderful day like today would have a crisis in the middle of it.

Just not this crisis.

Any crisis would be fine except this one.

Patty and I were both dressed in casual jeans and light shirts to spend the day together, since she had a day off from her job at the MGM Grand Hotel front desk. I still had on my black leather coat and fedora-like hat that was my uniform as a superhero. I just didn't feel comfortable going many places without them.

We had plans to tour the Mob Museum that both of us had wanted to see for a year, but hadn't found the time. Then we hoped to have a nice dinner and then go back to her apartment, watch a movie, and see what happened next.

I had been looking forward to that "next" part of the plan all morning.

And lunch in my office had seemed like a great way to start a relaxing and fun day together.

My invisible office floated a thousand feet over the Las Vegas Strip and consisted of four walls of windows and a diner booth smack in the middle of the room. The red vinyl booth had soft seats and could hold eight around the table with room enough for another two to pull up chairs on the end. It was patterned after Madge's imitation 1960's diner my team had met in for years down near Fremont Street in downtown Las Vegas.

An invisible door led from Madge's Diner to this office so that Madge, the waitress (who was also a superhero in the food service part of the gods) could wait on us in here. It was also the entrance for those without teleportation powers.

My office actually served as more of a clubhouse for the members of my team more than anything else. Sitting up here at night on a chair with your feet up on the railing looking out over the city and The Strip was always amazing and relaxing.

After hard days, a lot of the team members did just that.

There was also another invisible door that led to Patty's apartment where we stayed while in town. When we completed our new home we were building in the Oregon Coast Mountains, I would put in a direct door to this office from there as well.

Since Patty didn't teleport, that would allow her to get back to Vegas anytime she wanted from our new home in Oregon.

Patty Ledgerwood, aka Front Desk Girl, was my sidekick

and partner and the woman of my heart. We met the first time The Slots of Saturn ghost slots had attacked the city. And we had been a pair ever since.

Now it seemed the ghost slots were back.

Not possible, just not possible.

I just wasn't going to let myself believe it yet.

Madge came through the door from the diner with my cheeseburger and Patty's salad and a big basket of fries. She had already brought us both a large vanilla milkshake to share and had Stan's favorite strawberry shake on her tray as well.

She slid lunches in front of us and gave Stan his shake. Then she slid the fries over to an open spot at the end of the table and turned to leave without saying a word.

The fries only meant one thing. Laverne, Lady Luck herself, was on the way and had ordered ahead.

So the ghost slots really were back, even though that was completely impossible.

A moment later Screamer, the other original member of our team, and Ben, the oldest and yet newest member of our team appeared and slid into the other side of the booth facing me and Patty.

Screamer had taken part when we rescued over a hundred people from near death in the Slots of Saturn the first time. But wow, that was a long time ago.

Ten years ago, to be exact.

Screamer had the ability, among other things, to get into someone's head and read their thoughts and transfer those thoughts to others. He was a superhero working on the law enforcement side of the gods.

Ben was a god himself, just as Stan was. Ben had been the God of Lamplighters for centuries, but as they didn't need lamplighters as a profession anymore, he had faded. He had spent a lot of time over centuries reading and he remembered every detail. I got him moved over to work with the Gods of Books and Libraries to get him healthy again, and he had became a critical part of our team. He knew history and he knew all the politics and history of the gods. I couldn't believe how much he had helped us so far.

"So what Stan said is true?" I asked, looking at Screamer.

"We got ten people missing so far," Screamer said, nodding, "and my sources with the police think it might be a few more."

"But how?" Patty asked, her voice sounding as stunned as I felt. "We all three stood there outside that warehouse and watched those three slot machines be hauled off to be crushed and destroyed."

I glanced at Stan, who only shrugged. "We don't know, but we've seen security images of the Slots of Saturn appearing and taking someone and vanishing. Just as they did the first time. Exactly, actually. Same spots in the casinos. The locations they appear, that we know about, we now have blocked off."

"So they really are back?" I asked, the fear crushing any idea I had of taking a bite out of my cheeseburger, no matter how good it smelled.

"It seems that way," Stan said. "And we checked and they are not returning to the old Standard Machines warehouse."

"So we don't have any idea where they are stored this time?" I asked. That was how we had managed to deal with them the first time. We found their home.

"No clue at all," Lady Luck said, appearing and pulling a chair up to the table. She didn't grab a fry, but instead just sat there, staring at me.

And when Lady Luck just stares at you, that is not a good sign.

CHAPTER 2

SEARCHING FOR A CLUE IN
THE PAST

Ghost slots had been a myth or urban legend in Las Vegas since slot machines started to become popular. The myth was that a person could pour their entire soul into the machine and thus vanish into the machine.

In other words, slot machines took the souls of people.

I had walked by enough people glassy-eyed in front of slot machines over the decades to think there was some gems of truth in those legends.

And then ten years ago I discovered ghost slots were very, very real when the Slots of Saturn started to attack.

The Slots of Saturn were a three-seat set of very old, very tall slot machines with incredibly-beautiful images of the rings of Saturn all over the machines. You actually had to pull the handle and coins rattled out into the metal tray when you

9

won. They were old machines, retired in the late 1980s and stored in a giant warehouse called a "graveyard."

That's where we had found them through an incredible series of lucky events and teamwork. That day the team had managed to save over a hundred people from the ghost slots.

And we thought we had killed the slots.

Seems we hadn't.

The next two hours we all sat there in the booth, trying to figure out what to do next.

A couple times Lady Luck popped out to check on something, and Stan at one point agreed to talk with the Bookkeeper to see if he could get projections on the machines, assuming no one was controlling them.

Stan said the Bookkeeper was working on it when he came back and would call if he got some results.

The Bookkeeper was a god in the numbers area who never left his house or his computers. He could work a computer and research through the internet faster than anyone in existence. And he had an amazing talent of projecting events that would happen in the future using just numbers.

If someone had learned how to control those deadly slot monsters, then nothing the Bookkeeper could do to project their appearance would help. But if, like the first time, they were just runaway machines hungry for power from those who fed them, aka humans, then they could be predicted.

And the Bookkeeper could do it.

When they took a human, they jumped back to their original location. Then on some hidden schedule that only the

Bookkeeper and all his computers could project, the machines would jump again to a location, wait for another victim to sit down and pull the old handle, then with the victim trapped inside the machine, jump back to their original location.

The one limitation ghost slots had was that they could only go back to a place they had occupied in a casino at some point in the past. The problem was that in those days, slots were moved around from casino to casino all the time.

Records of slot movements were hard to find, hard to follow, or had been destroyed by now. There just didn't seem to be much of a reason to save where old slot machines had been thirty or forty or fifty years before and in old buildings now torn down.

Finally, after two hours, Patty and I and Ben were the only three left in the booth. Madge had long since taken away my partially eaten cheeseburger and brought Patty and me another vanilla milkshake.

Lady Luck had jumped off to talk with the gods of law enforcement to see what the real total of missing people might be.

And from exactly where.

Screamer had gone with Stan to talk with the only remaining slot machine tech who had been part of that rescue ten years before. The slot repairman who had triggered the first attack of the Slots of Saturn was now dead.

The three of us were in a wait-and-think mode.

Ben looked like anyone's standard image of the perfect grandfather. Short and square, dressed in a suit without a tie, with short gray hair and a receding hairline. He had a smile that could disarm anyone and now, after a year of working in the area of books and libraries, he had regained his strength from the centuries of being drained in the disappearance of his old job of being the God of Lamplighters.

I sipped on the remains of the milkshake and figured Patty and I needed to order something from Madge pretty soon to keep our strength up. Patty had barely touched her lunch salad as well.

Ben hadn't eaten a thing, even though I offered to buy him something a couple of times.

Patty was sitting beside me, but staring off out the window at a Southwest airliner making an approach into the airport.

"You know," Ben said. "Part of the solution to this might be in how you dealt with these monsters the first time."

"I've been thinking the same thing," I said. "But nothing we did back then seems to matter much this time around. At least not until we find their home and if they are being controlled."

Patty nodded to that.

"So I heard," Ben said, "that you two met fighting these slots. Is that right?"

Patty nodded and smiled, touching my leg, which always calmed me and excited me in a wonderful way, and this touch was no exception.

"We met slightly before we started working on beating the

Slots," I said, smiling and putting my hand over Patty's hand on my leg, "but yes, it was the event that pulled us together."

"So tell me about the meeting," Ben said. "I'm becoming sort of the unofficial historian for the gods, and since you two and your team have saved us all a number of times, it seems logical for me to know how all this started."

I honestly didn't know what to say. I wasn't sure how this would help us find the ghost slots, but at this point I trusted Ben and he seemed to think it might be a good use of our time.

Besides, there wasn't one damn thing I could think to do otherwise at the moment.

"You tell your side, first," Poker Boy," Ben said. "Then Patty, you can tell your side of the event."

"The first meeting?" I asked, glancing at Patty. "I honestly can't see how this will help."

"The first meeting," Ben said. "If it doesn't trigger something, then at least it will kill some time here while we wait."

I nodded and sat back. With Patty's hand on my leg, I let myself remember that first meeting with the woman of my life.

CHAPTER 3

THE MEMORY OF THAT FIRST MEETING

I love casinos. Always have.

I mean I truly love them, like some people enjoy sitting beside a calm mountain lake. Walking into a casino, it feels like I've stepped on an ocean beach on a warm evening with no wind, combined with the at-home feel of sitting by a fire, under a nice reading light, with a warm drink and a good book.

I admit, casinos are loud, with both machine and people noises, and are designed by experts to take a person's money. Yet every time I step through the door into a casino, either in Vegas, Atlantic City, or in Timbuck-six North Dakota, I know I am home, that I am safe, that I am in control of my surroundings.

As I stepped through the side door of the Horseshoe that day ten years ago, I walked right into the center of at least

15

forty poker tables. I knew at once I had once again found my own little slice of heaven.

I could feel the power flowing through me. My muscles, tense and tight from the long plane and cab ride, relaxed as if rubbed by a Swedish hot-rub expert.

Now remember, at that point I had only been in the superhero ranks for less than five years, and Stan had pretty much let me go on my own after a little talk or two. So green doesn't begin to describe me when it comes to all this god stuff. I'm still that way.

Ben waved for me to continue, so I did.

I remember that day stopping and just taking a deep breath of the smoke-tainted air of the old casino, filling my lungs with the poisons that killed others, but gave me strength.

Stopping just inside a casino front door was a habit of mine. Still is when I have time.

That day I remember clearly that everything around me looked like a standard day in casino world. And I had no sense that anything was off.

On my right were some of the live poker games, on my left the overflow part of the tournament area, now with all the tables empty. The main desk for the hotel was beyond all the tables, and I had to get there by sort of following the yellow brick road of the pattern on the carpet, through the tables, down between the railings along the live poker tables, and then through the ropes in the open area in front of the hotel desk.

Those ropes that guard the front desks of most hotels and ticket counters in airports always make me feel like a cow being herded to the guy with the hammer who would hit me, put me out of my misery, and turn my body into prime rib and flank steaks. I'm fairly certain some hotels have almost done that to me in the past.

There wasn't anyone waiting in line to check in at that moment. I remember clearly thinking that maybe I could avoid the ropes altogether and just go for the hammer.

I remember putting my head down and moving toward the front desk, pulling my suitcase behind me like a bad child, following the pattern on the carpet, hoping I could get checked in quickly and then take a nap.

I was there for the World Series of Poker which at that point was still held at Binion's Horseshoe Casino. I remember I somehow made it all the way to the front desk without stopping.

"Good afternoon, sir," I remember the woman behind the front desk saying as I stepped up to the polished wood counter.

I remember looking up and honestly, from that point things get a little fuzzy. It was Patty. I remember her smile actually included her brown eyes as she leaned forward a little. And what eyes they are.

"Thank you," Patty said and squeezed my hand.

Ben motioned that I continue and I did.

I think I remember having an out-of-body experience as I studied her eyes.

I knew I could stare into those eyes forever, but I knew I shouldn't.

Yet I remember wanting to.

I remember floating there, arguing with myself, until I finally returned to my body.

"Checking in," I remember that I managed to say, even though my throat was suddenly dry.

"Here for the tournament?" she asked me in return.

I remember saying I was and asking if it was that obvious?

"Poker players do have a look about them," she said to me.

I was in lust with Miss Brown-eyes behind the front desk. I wouldn't learn her name was Patty until later that day.

I gave her one of my many false travel names.

After a moment she said, "Here is your key," and slid the paper packet with the plastic key toward me. I reached for it and her hand brushed mine.

I remember seeing stars!

She wished me, I think, good luck with the tournament, and I thanked her somehow, I think.

Then I turned and tripped over my luggage.

I managed to miss getting tangled in the front desk rope maze as I fell.

That floor may have been carpeted, but I remember it was still hard, and it still hurt.

I remember she leaned over the desk and looked down at me like an angel, the light behind her head giving her a halo, and asked if I was all right.

I thought of staying down, staring at her until she floated over to help me up, then thought better of it.

I sprang to my feet and I somehow managed to not sprint for the elevators.

I looked at Ben and Patty and shrugged. "My side of that first meeting."

Patty squeezed my leg. "You were so cute."

"Falling down was cute?" I asked.

"It was," she said, smiling at me with that same smile I had come to love for ten years.

"So, Patty," Ben said, "tell me your side of what happened."

I looked at her because I realized that in ten years I had never heard her side of that story.

"I knew Poker Boy was coming in for the tournament," Patty said. "And I spotted you at once when you came through the door and stopped. I thought you were cute before you did the dive over the luggage."

"You did?" I asked, stunned.

"Of course," she said, again squeezing my leg. "I had heard a few things about how you had saved some people and a few dogs and stopped Stan from losing his job and all that. So I wanted to meet you."

"Did you know about the Slots of Saturn at that point?" Ben asked Patty.

Patty nodded, which stunned me.

"My boss, Bernice, the God of Hospitality, had been dealing with the missing persons reports all over town. She and I both had a hunch we were dealing with ghost slots, but I honestly didn't want to believe it. None of us did at that point. It was better to think of a more realistic reason than something like ghost slots."

Ben nodded.

I just sat there, surprised.

"So when did you realize you were actually dealing with ghost slots?"

Patty looked at me. "When you and I saw them on the security tape take a customer from the Binion's gaming floor."

I nodded. "That's a memory I'm not going to soon forget."

In fact, just the memory of it right now had me sweating a little.

CHAPTER 4

ANOTHER TRIP TO FIND A CLUE IN THE PAST

Ben asked us a few more questions about that second meeting and why we took Samantha, the blind wife of the man who was taken by the slots from Binion's, out of the hotel and to Madge's Diner.

That decision had started our regular meetings for years in the diner and then the design of this office when I built it two years ago.

Going to Madge's had been Patty's idea and my idea to bring in Screamer to help.

Ben walked us all the way through the entire events of that first battle, how we found the slots in the old Standard Slots Graveyard warehouse and how we rescued the people from inside the slots.

Then he asked a very simple question, one that I had a

hunch he had been working to for the entire last half hour. "So when was the last time you saw the ghost slots?"

"I remember it clearly," I said. "It was hot, middle of the afternoon."

"A Tuesday," Patty said. "With Screamer, we watched as the two hauling men and two men from Standard Slots hauled the big monster out of the warehouse and craned it up onto a flatbed truck."

"They covered it with tarps and tied it down," I said. "We stood and talked to the Standard men as the two haulers left with it on the back of their truck, headed supposedly to the crusher out at the wrecking yard to the east of town."

Then it dawned on me what I had said. We had a trail, but a ten-year-old trail.

"The truck drivers kept the machine, didn't they?" I said to Ben. "We need to find them and where they kept it the last ten years, or who they sold it to, and we'll have our home for the machines."

I turned to Patty. "You remember the name of the trucking company by any chance? It had a logo on the door."

"Steven's Hauling," Patty said without hesitation.

Damn her memory never ceased to amaze me.

I grabbed my cell phone and dialed The Bookkeeper. Of all the people I knew, he was the best with computers and the internet and research than anyone.

"Still no schedule yet," the Bookkeeper said when he answered the phone.

"Can you trace Steven's Hauling?" I asked. "They picked up the slots ten years ago from the old graveyard warehouse.

"Call you right back," he said.

I hung up and then said, "Stan, we might have a lead."

A moment later Stan appeared with Screamer.

"We're tracking the company that hauled away the slots," I said to him.

"We were trying to find that information out," Stan said, "but the Standard Warehouse Records were long gone. How did you figure it out just sitting here?"

"A short trip down memory lane for Ben," I said, "and Patty's great memory of the name on the truck. Steven's Hauling. I got the Bookkeeper tracing it."

My phone rang.

I answered it and the Bookkeeper said, "Steven's Hauling has been out of business since 2010 when one of their trucks wrecked on the way to LA, killing both of the brothers who owned the company and did all the work of hauling off the slots back ten years ago. Three days after hauling the slots from the warehouse, they deposited three thousand in cash into their bank account that they didn't account for. That was about the going rate for an old set of slots like that back then."

"Nothing else?" I asked.

"All the company records were destroyed in 2012. Now, I'm going back to trying to figure out where these monsters are going to land next."

With that he hung up.

I looked at Patty and Ben and Stan and Screamer. "Dead

end. No record of who they sold it to and the brothers who owned and worked the company are dead and all records destroyed."

"And more bad news," Screamer said. "We've got twelve missing so far."

"That the police know about," Stan said.

All I could do was take a deep breath and just wonder what in the world we were going to do to stop this.

Again.

Chapter 5

Got Them!

Patty and I were just about to jump to her apartment, change clothes, and head out for a quiet dinner so we could think when Screamer got a call.

He listened for a moment, then said, "Be right there."

He slipped the phone back into his pocket and said, "Slots of Saturn are in Binion's. Same spot as ten years ago. Police have them surrounded, so no unsuspecting customer is going to jump them at the moment."

Instead of teleporting into a dead camera area, it was just as easy for us to head down through Madge's Diner entrance to my office, out the front door, and across the street to Binion's.

The three slot machines that had haunted my dreams for ten years were there, right where Patty and I had seen them on the security tape all those years ago.

And they looked exactly the same. Exactly.

Bright colors, the images of Saturn and the rings cutting across all three machines, three wooden chairs attached in front of them.

My nightmare had returned in bright, living color.

They were pulsing, dim to bright, every second or so, and I could sense the pull they were putting on people around them, including the police.

Including me.

They were hungry and if they didn't find a victim soon, they might jump.

And when they did, we needed to somehow trace them.

I dropped us all out of time, freezing everything around us. I loved that superpower almost as much as I loved the ability to teleport. All I had actually done was take me and Patty and Ben and Screamer and Stan between instants of time.

But all the casino sounds and the sounds coming from Fremont Street stopped instantly. Also, I could thankfully no longer feel the pull from the slots.

"That thing feels like it's about to jump," I said.

Stan nodded and an instant later Laverne appeared wearing her most distinct black power business suit and her hair pulled back tight. A different look than the last time she had been in my office.

"Got any ideas?" she said, staring at the slots.

"It's about to jump, even if it doesn't get fed," I said. "Do we have anyone who can trace that amount of energy through time and space to figure out where it goes?"

There was a long moment of silence inside an already deadly quiet time bubble.

Then Screamer looked at me, then Stan, and Lady Luck. "Is that machine pouring out a lot of energy?"

"It is," Lady Luck said. "And the energy feels very much human, so like the last time, the thing is being powered by the people inside it."

Screamer then said something that surprised me. "We need Sherri here."

Now Sherri was one of Lady Luck's four daughters and Screamer's wife. They had been separated for some time, a couple of decades from what I understood. But Screamer and Sherri had been working slowly to try to figure out a way to be together. I always knew when he and Sherri had spent time together because he came back smiling.

But at the moment Sherri, who was a superhero, was tending bar in Reno and working for the Gods of Food and Beverage.

She had offered to be part of the team, but until this moment, none of us ever thought to get her involved in any problem.

"Why Sherri?" Lady Luck said a moment before I could.

"She's developed in the last year or so an ability to sense and follow energy," Screamer said. "She can trace a person's energy through a building hours after they walked through it.

I think she might be able to trace those monsters, since it's powered by human energy."

Screamer pointed to the frozen ghost slots.

"Didn't know that," Lady Luck said, nodding. "Interesting new type of superpower. Worth a shot. Hold this time bubble and we'll go get her."

Screamer and Lady Luck vanished.

"Did you know Sherri could do that?" I asked both Stan and Patty and Ben.

All of them shook their heads.

"Might be a good power to add into the mix at times," Patty said.

"We shall see," I said, nodding. But I agreed with her. I could think of a couple times that might have been very handy.

An instant later Lady Luck, Screamer, and Sherri appeared.

Sherri was wearing basically the same thing she had on the first time I had met her. Tan slacks, white blouse, and an Eldorado bar apron. She had her long, pitch-black hair pulled back tight, which just accented her stunning beauty.

She and Screamer were holding hands, so I was pretty sure he had transferred to her what was happening. And all the background that had happened ten years ago. He could do that with a touch, let her see inside his head what was happening.

As they appeared, she stepped forward, staring at the Slots

of Saturn. "So these are the ghost slots you three defeated ten years ago?"

"They are," Screamer said. "Same damn ones exactly."

"Let's see if I can trace them or not," she said. "Drop the time bubble."

I did as she asked and the sounds of the casino crashed back in around us.

Instantly the wave of energy powered over us from the pulsing slots.

Sherri staggered back into Screamer's arms and collapsed as the slots pulsed faster and faster and faster and then vanished, leaving a newer bunch of slots in its place.

I glanced back at Sherri.

She was out cold and both Screamer and Lady Luck were hovering over her.

A moment later all three of them vanished.

"I'll find out how she's doing," Stan said, and vanished as well, leaving me and Ben and Patty just standing there.

"I think I need a rest," Ben said. "I'll catch up with everyone later."

He vanished.

I looked around at the cops and the people who had been watching all this. And watching all of us just vanish out of thin air. I had no idea how anyone was going to explain all this, or if they would even try, but right at that moment I didn't care.

I jumped Patty and me back to the bedroom of her apartment and stretched out on the bed, not even bothering to take off my leather coat. I used my hat to shade my eyes from what little light was coming around the long drapes pulled closed over the window.

Patty stretched out beside me and took my hand.

"We'll figure it out," she said softly.

I just wished I believed her, because if we didn't, a lot of people were going to die a very ugly death inside a very nasty machine.

Chapter 6

A Nightmare

I dozed, lying there on the bed.

In the dream, I was back in that old Standard Warehouse, and Patty and I and Screamer were madly trying to save people as the big machine spit them out, one per second.

Patty had slowed down time just enough that, as the people appeared, Screamer could shove them out of the way onto a big tarp. It had taken us a couple hours to get everyone out that way, with a few problems, but we had done it.

And then the memory dream turned to a nightmare as the ghosts of the people we had saved just wandered the old warehouse full of dead slot machines, not knowing where to go.

And no one would believe they were there.

I woke up with a jerk, sweating.

Patty had gone into the bathroom and was taking a shower.

I lay there, letting my heart slow down, trying to figure out what that dream was all about.

And coming up with nothing.

Ghost slots. Ghost people. That made no sense at all.

Then my cell phone rang. "Sherri's fine," Screamer said. "Meet in your office in an hour for dinner?"

"We'll be there," I said.

I took off my coat and hat and then the rest of my clothes. The nightmare had caused me to sweat right through them.

I headed into the bathroom and crawled into the large shower with Patty, who kissed me, then climbed out.

"What fun is that?" I asked, teasing her, even though I had no intention of fooling around.

"Lot of time for fun when we find those damn machines," she said. "And hurry up, I've got an idea I want to check out."

"Sherri is all right," I said as the cool water rinsed over me, chasing some of the nightmare away. "We're meeting in the office in an hour for dinner."

"Perfect," Patty said, heading out to get dressed.

Twenty minutes later I jumped us across town to a secluded spot near the front gate of an old wrecking yard.

The heat from the desert slammed in on us like a hammer. It always seemed hot in the city, but out in the desert, it always felt worse. And jumping from a comfortable air-conditioned apartment into the direct sun and heat wasn't fun. Especially wearing a black leather coat.

I looked around to make sure we hadn't been spotted. There was no one to see us. The place was acres of dead cars in a small valley to the east of Las Vegas, hidden from sight from just about anything. Sitting in long rows, the old and wrecked cars seemed to just be waiting patiently to be picked apart by car enthusiasts like vultures over dried bones.

A wooden building just inside the open chain-link gate served as an office. They were clearly open. Beyond the office was a huge machine that was in the process of crushing a car, making a noise I didn't want to really listen to for very long. At least not without some great earplugs.

We headed up the dusty gravel road and then into the wooden building that looked like it hadn't been painted since the area was settled.

The door creaked as we went in and a bell rang, as if the door creaking wasn't enough to shout that someone had entered. The cool insides of the office felt like I had dipped my face into a cold drink. We were greeted by an elderly woman who had to be in her seventies. She had on a nametag that read, "Denise" that looked like she was attending a convention more than working in a dusty office in the middle of nowhere.

The place smelled of auto parts and oil and grease, and there were pictures of racing cars on the walls and a large glass case full of trophies, some of which looked to be fifty years old. Some of the pictures jammed all over the walls were clearly of Denise in much younger and thinner days.

"What can I do for you kids?" Denise asked as she climbed to her feet and headed toward us from her cluttered desk.

"We're wondering if your smashing records still go back ten years," Patty asked, giving Denise her best smile and charm that was part of her superpower at front desks.

Patty could calm the most angry customer with a wave of energy and a smile. I could feel the waves of it coming off of her now.

"Oh, sure, dear," Denise said, her voice sounding like a grandmother's voice right out of the movies. "We have records back for forty years since we bought the Big Bully, as we call the noisy old thing."

"Any chance you might have records of crushing an antique three-chair set of slots ten years ago, almost to the day, give or take a few?"

"Let me check," Denise said.

She went to some huge metal filing cabinets that lined the back wall and stretched down one side of a hallway that led to a back office and bathroom.

I wasn't sure exactly what Patty was thinking, because if the slots never arrived here, we were still at the same spot. But I agreed with this search just to make sure they hadn't arrived here and then were sold from here.

Denise pulled open one drawer with a bang and thumbed

through a few files for a moment, then checked a few more, and pulled one file, shaking her head.

"We only crushed one slot grouping that entire year," Denise said. "I remember they were really nice-looking old slots owned by Standard, but the guys from the shipping company insisted they help us put them into Big Bully themselves to make sure they were destroyed. Something about them being haunted. It's in the notes here."

Denise shook her head again. "Can you believe haunted slots?"

Neither of us said a thing. I wasn't sure what I believed any more.

Then Denise slipped the manilla file folder across the counter toward Patty.

Patty looked at it and gasped.

I couldn't believe what I was seeing either.

Someone had taken a color Polaroid of the Slots of Saturn half crushed by two huge metal crushing arms of a big machine.

"We take a picture of everything we crush as it's being crushed," Denise said. "That way we're never accused of double-dipping like some crushing yards."

We said nothing. I was too stunned to say anything.

"That what you were looking for?" Denise asked. "Almost ten years to the day as you said."

"That's perfect, thanks," Patty said, pushing the file back to Denise. "Can you make us a copy of that?"

"Oh, sure," Denise said and took the thin file to a copy machine.

A couple minutes later we walked back out into the heat, Patty holding the copies of the file. The smell of desert and old cars hit me again as we walked down the slight hill on the old gravel road and through the big gate to get out of sight of anyone in the wrecking yard.

How could the slots have been destroyed?

I had just seen them at Binion's just a short few hours before.

"Are we dealing with real ghost slots this time?" Patty asked, her voice low and soft, as we walked through the heat.

"I honestly don't know," I said, feeling completely helpless as I jumped us back to my office overlooking Las Vegas.

I had no idea how to fight machines.

I really had no idea how to fight ghost machines.

CHAPTER 7

A SILENT DINNER

After Patty passed around the record from the wrecking yard and the picture, the dinner started off pretty silent. Stan, Ben, Screamer, and Sherri were there with us.

Screamer and Sherri were staying close and sometimes touching across from me in the booth. Ben sat in the back of the booth, saying little, and Stan sat in a chair at the end of the booth.

Madge came and went with food and drinks, but said little. That was normal for her unless she had some observation and like the rest of us, she didn't seem to have many ideas on this mess.

So finally I asked Sherri what exactly she felt when the machine jumped and knocked her out.

"Like I had grabbed a supercharged electrical fence," she said, shaking her head. "Hurt like hell."

Screamer touched her arm and she smiled slightly. Somehow his power and touch must have eased the memory of the pain some.

"Could you tell what kind of energy it was?" Patty asked.

"Human energy," Sherri said without hesitation. "The same kind of energy I can track long after a person goes by. Only multiplied by factors and focused."

"And any sense of the machine now?" Ben asked.

She shook her head. "Nothing. It just vanished."

"Do you think if it was here, you would be able to sense it?"

"I'm sure of it," she said. "And I think I'll know the instant it comes back anywhere in town."

"Well," I said, nodding to myself. "That's going to help."

And I really believed it might. I wasn't sure how, but knowing when it arrived, even if in a place the police didn't have protected, would help a lot.

Screamer smiled at Sherri. "That's what I said."

"I hope so," Sherri said.

At that point Madge brought everyone dinner. This was not the nice, quiet dinner Patty and I had hoped to have, but there were people's lives at stake. We could always go out to a better dinner on another day.

I had ordered deep-fried shrimp. Patty again had some kind of a salad, only with chicken on it.

We all ate pretty much in silence, and I was almost

through my shrimp and baked potato when Lady Luck arrived and pulled up a chair next to Stan, who scooted over to give her room.

"Feeling better?" she asked Sherri.

Sherri nodded. "I am, thanks. Any leads?"

Lady Luck shook her head and a moment later Madge appeared and slid a salad similar to Patty's in front of one of the most powerful gods in the world.

We all went back to eating in silence.

I just kept running down everything I could think of, and I kept coming up blank. Then I remembered the Bookkeeper who had been trying to predict the machines.

"Stan, have you checked with the Bookkeeper?" I asked.

He shook his head. "Just makes him angry when I push him."

"Don't you think he needs to know the machines were destroyed ten years ago?"

Stan nodded and took out his cell phone, standing to move off to talk with the Bookkeeper.

Lady Luck looked at me with that stare of hers again, the one that could melt a normal person and pretty much did to me. I couldn't imagine what it must have been like for her daughters to grow up with that look.

"Destroyed?" Lady Luck asked.

I nodded and Patty took the copies of the file from beside her and handed them to Lady Luck.

"Son of a bitch," Lady Luck said after a moment of looking inside, then handing the file back to Patty.

I didn't know she swore like that.

Then Lady Luck took another forkful of her salad, stuffed it in her mouth, and vanished.

As we all sat there, sort of in shock at Lady Luck swearing, Stan came back over to the table and sat down. "The Book-keeper was swearing at me when he hung up."

"Mom just did the same thing," Sherri said, shaking her head. "That's not a good thing when Mom swears."

When Mom was Lady Luck, there was no chance in the world I was going to disagree with that.

CHAPTER 8

ANOTHER ENCOUNTER

Ten minutes later not a one of us could figure why both Lady Luck and the Bookkeeper were so upset about the machines having been destroyed ten years before.

"There's something none of us know," Stan said, "that they clearly do and don't really want to tell us yet."

I couldn't argue with that, but as a lowly superhero, I was sort of used to either being in the dark, or just flat uninformed. I didn't like it, but I had gotten used to the feeling. It was why I liked having Ben around. He helped me with the history.

I turned to him with that thought. "Any record of anything like this happening before?"

"Nothing," he said. "Nothing even close in thousands of years of my memory."

Suddenly, Sherri tipped forward and grabbed her head.

Screamer instantly held her, clearly working to help her in some fashion, his eyes closed.

After a moment I asked softly, "Need help?"

"Patty," he said.

Patty reached across the booth without hesitation and touched Sherri's arm and then closed her eyes.

At that moment I knew all three of them were linked up for some reason. And I had a hunch I knew what the reason was.

The machines were back in town from wherever they went.

And Screamer and Patty were helping Sherri set up some mental shields against the intense energy.

Finally, after what seemed like a very long time, but must have only been fifteen seconds, Patty sat back and released her touch on Sherri.

"Machines are back at Binion's again," Patty said.

Sherri sat up straight and opened her eyes. They looked a little haunted, but not bad.

"Thanks," she said to Screamer and Patty. "I can deal with them now if I don't get too close."

Screamer's phone rang and he answered it. Then after a moment he said, "Make sure no one goes near them."

"Police still have the area surrounded," Screamer said. "So we won't lose another person this time."

"Think from this distance you might be able to follow the machines this time when they jump?" I asked Sherri.

She nodded. "With Patty and Screamer's help I can try."

Patty slipped out of the booth and slid in on the other side with Sherri and Screamer. I watched from across the expanse of empty plates and used drinking glasses as the three of them got ready.

I felt helpless. But I knew that sometimes a leader of a group was best left observing. I didn't like it, but I knew that to be the case now.

All three of their minds were going to be linked.

"It's powering up to jump," Sherri said.

Screamer held her shoulders and Patty reached over and held onto Sherri's arm.

All three of them closed their eyes, clearly no longer mentally in the booth.

After four or five seconds, all three of them jerked as if shocked. Then they slumped.

I wanted to shout to see if Patty was all right, but somehow I held my panic under control slightly.

Finally Patty opened her eyes, looking at me and smiling at what must have been a panicked look on my face.

"Could you trace them?" Stan asked.

Patty shook her head and took a deep breath.

"We should have been able to follow them," Sherri said, opening her eyes as well and looking at Stan. "Anywhere on the planet. But it was as if the surge shut them off as they vanished."

Screamer nodded agreement and handed Sherri a glass of water.

"We never saw them shut off ten years ago," I said. "So is there any place on this planet you couldn't trace them to?"

"Nowhere," Sherri said, and beside her Screamer again nodded in agreement. He had been inside her head, he knew what she felt and saw as well.

Suddenly Lady Luck was back at the end of the table.

She pulled up a chair, still clearly upset. "You are both right and wrong, daughter. There is no place on this planet you could not have traced them to with your power and the help of your husband and Patty."

"So where are they?" I asked.

"They are on this planet," Lady Luck said, looking at me. "Just not in this timeline."

Lady Luck took a forkful of the salad still sitting in front of her. And before putting it in her mouth she added, "and not in this time period either."

CHAPTER 9

A TIME HEADACHE

I hated any thought of time travel. It always gave me a headache.

And now just mentioning it again felt like it might give me one again.

Patty stood and stretched and then came around and slid back into the booth beside me. She touched me and I could feel she was tired, drained from her experience with Sherri and Screamer.

I focused some energy in her direction through our contact and she smiled, letting the energy in so that she could regain some strength. I liked that about our relationship. Together we were a lot, lot stronger than alone.

Before I could even formulate a question for Lady Luck, Stan's phone rang.

"Bookkeeper," Stan said, and answered the phone without leaving the table.

"Yeah," Stan said. "We know that."

Then he listened for a moment and I watched his face. It wasn't easy to get a read on the God of Poker, but sometimes when Stan wasn't aware, he let down his guard. And this was one of those times.

His eyebrows seemed to creep up his forehead toward his receding hairline as he clearly got news he didn't want to hear.

Then he asked, "How long?"

"Thanks," Stan said after a moment. "Anything else, call me."

He clicked off his cell phone and looked at the silent group around the table.

"We have fourteen hours," Stan said, "to solve this."

"I was afraid of that," Lady Luck said. "That's what Kronos told me as well."

Kronos, the God of Time, was the only one allowed to travel in time. He controlled it and if he thought this was a problem, it really was a problem.

"What happens in twenty-three hours?" Sherri asked.

"This timeline we are in is permanently separated from our original timeline," Stan said.

Lady Luck and Ben were both shaking their heads, clearly understanding what that meant.

And knowing what he meant.

I had no clue. Not one.

And I could tell the other superheroes at the table had no

idea what the gods were saying or thinking, since there were blank looks on the faces I could see. I could feel my look was as puzzled as the rest.

"What happens then?" Screamer asked.

"This entire timeline drops into a time loop," Lady Luck said.

"A what?" Screamer asked a moment before I could get out the question.

"Think Groundhog's Day, the movie," Stan said, "only we won't have a memory of anything repeating."

"This timeline would just repeat the last few days," Lady Luck said flatly, "plus the next fourteen hours over and over and over. We would never know it and never escape."

My stomach clamped up so tight I wasn't sure if I could even swallow. And my lungs seemed to expel every ounce of breath they were holding.

That was the worst kind of jail I could ever imagine.

"How do we know," I asked, afraid of the question, "that we didn't fail and are already in a time loop?"

"We don't," Lady Luck said. "So let's not fail, because I don't want to eat this salad for the rest of eternity."

CHAPTER 10

A TICKING CLOCK

After we all sat there for a few long moments in silence, thinking about our possible eternities having dinner together, the same dinner, and not knowing we were doing it, I finally managed to get a thought in my brain and let it come out my mouth.

"What caused this in the first place?"

"You did," Stan said.

"We all did," Lady Luck corrected. "None of us knew. We were just glad Poker Boy and Patty and Screamer saved the gambling industry, remember?"

"I'm not following," I said.

"We saved people the machine had taken from this time-line and just left them in the past," Patty said.

Now I knew that didn't sound good.

Stan nodded. "So to get those same people again, the

49

machine has to jump to another timeline and take the same people again and again and again. Jumping from timeline to timeline. A time loop creating new alternate realities off the same event."

"So we already saved everyone who is in the machine the first time?" I asked.

"You did," Lady Luck said, nodding. "Now we have to save all the rest of us and everyone in this timeline."

"So the main timeline actually got split back ten years ago?" Screamer asked.

Lady Luck nodded.

"So to stop this," I asked. "Will Kronos allow us to go back in time and fix the mistake?"

"He will," Lady Luck said. "I already asked him and he agreed if I went along. We can bring the victims back to the future and that will reset all the timelines."

I could feel my stomach starting to unclamp. "So what's the problem?"

She looked at me. "Do you know which people you saved were from that past time and which were from this time?"

"Oh," Patty said, slumping slightly beside me.

"We don't have a lot of time to figure that out," I said. "We can do that, can't we?"

Lady Luck nodded. "We can, but if we miss one, we're into the time loop and will always miss one."

She was so full of good news I couldn't stand it.

She stood. "I've got some things to set up, and I need to talk with Kronos again."

She vanished.

I took a deep breath and pushed the headache back. We needed to get moving and move fast. I turned to Stan. "Can you get the Bookkeeper on this?"

"He said he would start the computer searches for them when I talked with him. He should have a list for us shortly."

I nodded. "We don't want to trust it, though." I looked at Stan again. "Can you talk with the gods in charge of the police and get a full list of names we rescued?"

"I'll get it," Stan nodded and vanished.

"So what do we do?" Screamer asked.

I sat there staring at the four left around the table that was still covered with our dinner dishes. Then it suddenly dawned on me that we had yet another way of getting information.

We could travel back without actually traveling in time.

"Screamer, when you pushed those people out of the chair, you touched them."

"I did," he said, frowning at me. "Do you really think after ten years that I can remember flashes of who they all were just from touching them for an instant?"

"I do," I said, smiling at my friend. "With help. Whatever we get can work as another check-point to make sure the lists we get are 100% accurate."

"I don't know how I could do that," Screamer said, shaking his head.

"It won't just be you," I said. "Remember, all three of us were hooked up and thus all three of us caught a glimpse of the mind of each person you touched."

"Good point," Patty said, "But I don't think I remember much either."

"I remember us being a little busy," Screamer said.

"But we have a secret weapon."

I looked directly into the wonderful brown eyes of the love of my life. It took her a moment, but then she laughed, clearly understanding what I was getting at.

She smiled at me and then turned to Screamer. "Remember how I slowed the time down so we can get the people out of the chairs?"

Screamer nodded.

"I can slow the time down even more in memory. A lot more."

I looked at Ben, who just smiled at me and nodded his agreement.

"Ben can remember what we all only caught a glimpse of in each person," I said, "if he's linked to us when we go back into the memory."

Screamer nodded slowly. "You know, Poker Boy, that's a hairbrained scheme like most of your schemes, and it just might work."

I was sure hoping it would.

"And what am I going to do?" Sherri asked.

I looked at her and then at Screamer. "Keep all of us calm and focused, since that few hours we spent getting those people out was very traumatic for all of us, and will be hard to relive."

She looked at her husband and nodded. "I can do that."

"Ben," I said, turning to him, "are you going to be able to remember all the details we each see with each person we rescued?"

He laughed. "I promise, I won't miss a detail, no matter how small. But I suggest we do nine at a time, stop, and I relay everything I got to see if it matches what everyone remembers from the experience."

"Very good idea," I said. "That way we won't be totally stressed."

"Oh, we'll be stressed," Patty said. "I never thought I'd have to relive those hours of sheer terror again."

"I didn't either," Screamer said. "I had nightmares for years about bodies materializing inside of each other."

"We got to do this," I said, shuddering at the memory of that exact same nightmare. "And we have to get it right."

"Because if we don't," Screamer said, "we're destined to relive what we are about to try over and over and over inside a time loop."

"That's not a time loop," I said. "That's hell."

"I've been down on a visit to hell," Sherri said. "This would be worse."

Everyone but Screamer looked at her. I think I had my mouth open.

She looked around and smiled. "What? An old boyfriend is all. You know how kids are."

"Before my time," Screamer said, shaking his head.

Chapter 11

A Second Time Through A Nightmare

We told Madge what we were planning and she cleaned off the table and brought us all pads of paper and pens and some fresh glasses of water.

While she was doing that, Sherri and Screamer jumped to her mother to tell her the plan and I called to Stan to come back and I explained the plan to him.

Lady Luck and Stan both thought it was a good idea.

While we were getting set up, Stan got in the list from the Bookkeeper of the names and location his computers told him were the ones from the future we stranded in the past.

I wouldn't let Stan show it to us, since I didn't want what we were about to try to be contaminated in any way.

Stan thought that very smart and agreed. He jumped away

to continue to get help from the police on the overall list of names.

So as we all slipped into the booth, we put Screamer in the middle in the back. Sherri was on one side of him and Ben beside her.

Patty was on the other side of Screamer and I was beside her.

Patty and I and Screamer had had our minds together a lot over the years, but this was the first time we had tried it with both Sherri and Ben also in the mix.

"Stay focused on the memory," I said and everyone agreed.

"We start from the first one and go through?" Screamer asked.

"From the first one," I said and he nodded.

Why he had asked about the first one was because the first person out of the machine had been Geneva, a reporter from the *Las Vegas Sun* who we had sent in so that we could communicate with someone inside. She and her boyfriend, a cop friend of mine named Johnny, had developed a very tight mental connection that we used.

I wanted to make sure we didn't get confused in the order and miss anyone.

"Ready for a ride back to hell?" Screamer asked.

Patty and I both nodded.

Sherri took Ben's hand on top of the table and touched Screamer's leg with the other.

Patty touched my leg and then took Screamer's hand on top of the table.

Instantly there were four other people in my head.

I tried to only focus on my memory of that hot day in that graveyard of slot machines.

Patty and Screamer did the same and Sherri sent some waves of calming energy as we were again back in front of those monster machines ten years before.

Ben just felt like a shadow in the distance, watching.

The intense terror I felt overwhelmed me and I could feel Patty's and Screamer's fear as well.

We were standing right in front of the pulsating machines. I was touching Screamer and Patty was holding my hand.

I got the distinct smell of raspberry shampoo, but pushed that thought away and focused on what was about to happen.

Patty had slowed down time and then, slowly, in the chair in front of the right-side slot machine, a woman's body started to materialize seated in the wooden chair.

Screamer reached out when she was complete and shoved her hard out of the way.

I focused on her mind, what was in it, and caught a lot about her and her new relationship with Johnny. More than I thought I could get, actually.

The next person, a woman, started to materialize and I remember thinking how close that was and how fast that was happening, even with Patty slowing time.

Scary fast, Patty thought at me. *I had my eyes closed and hadn't realized it was that close. No wonder you and Screamer have nightmares of people materializing together.*

More than you want to know, Screamer thought at her.

As the woman finished materializing, Screamer pushed her hard out of the way and onto the mat beside the chair. She landed in slow motion on top of Geneva.

The woman's mind seemed open to me. I scanned as much as I could in the fraction of a second Screamer was in contact with her. I could see in her memory that when she was taken by the slots, there was a 2004 Mercedes spinning slowly on some progressive slot machine display to her right. And she was thinking she would really love to win that new car.

Casinos didn't give away old cars, so she was from that time, not today.

The next one out was Ben, the man Patty and I had seen taken from Binion's.

We knew he was fine as well.

Back then we had taken two minutes rests between every group of three, but we didn't need to do that in memory, so we jumped over the two minutes and went through the next three people out of the machine, then did that again with three more.

Then both Patty and Sherri broke their connection with Screamer as we planned.

"Wow, you three were terrified," Sherri said. "I'm impressed you managed to save all those people under that kind of stress and fear. And working with untested super-powers as well. Amazing."

"Thanks for keeping us calm this time through," Screamer said and leaned over and kissed her. "That was a lot better than the first time we had to live that."

I had to agree with him. Sherri was managing to keep the fear in all of us that we felt back then pushed back.

I turned to Ben. "Did you get it all?"

"Every detail," he said. "We start from the first person."

We all grabbed our papers and pens and Ben gave us the first person's full name and when she was born and how she had gotten taken.

We all agreed on the first one, that what he said matched what we saw as well.

He went on to the second woman, then on to Ben, detailing all three out.

Then he went to the next three, and again all three were taken in 2004. That much was clear, without a doubt.

On each person who it was clear was from 2004, I drew a line through their name on my pad.

It wasn't until we got to number eight out of the machine that we found our first person from this present time.

There was no doubt at all with him.

His name was Willie (William) Jamison. He had been taken as the last one from this time period. He had been twenty-one when taken.

"Oh, no," Patty said as Ben described him.

"What? I asked.

"Remember his face," Patty said. "Do you recognize it?"

"Oh, bloody hell," Screamer said, shaking his head.

I could picture the guy's face and it did look familiar, but darned if I could remember from where.

"He took on the name Ben Williams," Patty said, "back in 2004."

And then it flooded over me. Ben Williams had killed a middle-aged couple in a very brutal and angry fashion in what was called a home invasion. He was found covered in the couple's blood holding their twelve-year-old son. He was sentenced to life in prison and the press said he never showed remorse.

"He was an abused child," Ben said softly. "When he found himself stuck in the past, he had to save his younger self from his own parents."

"And that's why we have alternate realities," Lady Luck said, appearing in front of the booth. "Kronos didn't notice that one forming because it made so little impact, since his parents did nothing and in the main timeline will die not many years from now anyway."

"And the young Willie?" I asked, afraid of the answer.

"He killed himself in foster care at the age of sixteen."

"Keep up the good work," she said, nodding to the silence in the room and then vanishing.

We had one.

We had gone through only nine of over a hundred.

This really was hell. We just had to make sure we didn't miss anyone from this time so that we didn't repeat this hell into eternity.

No pressure.

CHAPTER 12

THE SWAMP OF PEOPLE'S LIVES

We made it through the next nine without finding anyone from our time. Of that I was 100 percent sure. With Patty slowing down even more the moment that Screamer had touched each person, we were all digging into each person's life.

And there was a lot of it I flat didn't want to dig into.

One was a child molester that when we went over it with our pens and paper, both Screamer and I made a note to look up to see if he was still alive.

Others had strange sexual habits that were not illegal, but made me look away. Others were buried in loneliness, others still were using gambling as a way to escape one ugly thing or another in their life. Of the nine, not a one of them was a happy person.

I'm not sure if that was a comment on slot players or just the luck of the draw.

As we finished with the third nine and came back to the present, Madge brought us all milkshakes and big baskets of hot fries. The vanilla milkshake tasted wonderful and the fries were perfect.

I didn't realize how much I needed both.

We again went over each name and it was number twenty-two that had come from today.

Penny Smith was her name. She had been widowed the year before at the age of fifty-four and was using gambling with slots to take her mind off her sorrow of losing the man of her life to cancer. I had no idea what she had done when she discovered she was trapped in the past, and I wasn't sure I wanted to know.

Screamer said the same thing.

Patty and Sherri said nothing.

Ben seemed to never make a comment on the people whose privacy we were invading.

So we had two after going through twenty-seven people.

We found the next one from this time two groups of nine later. Number forty-two.

She was a widower at thirty-five because her husband had been murdered. Actually, it was clear in her mind that she had murdered him for having an affair on her.

She had gotten all his money, played the grieving widow for a year or so, and then moved to Vegas last year.

"We'll deal with her after all this is settled," Screamer said, smiling at me.

I had no doubt he and the police would deal with her just fine. But after seeing the inside of that woman's evil mind, I wanted to help, or at least watch the police arrest her. She had already been plotting on finding her next rich husband when we stranded her in the past.

Beside me, Patty shuddered. "There is true evil out there, isn't there?"

I touched her arm and gave her energy to go on.

She smiled at me and said, "Thanks. Not so sure how I got so lucky to find someone like you."

"Raspberry shampoo," I said.

Screamer snorted and Patty had the decency to blush.

I had a clear memory of being in lust with Patty right from the first time I saw her. But all these trips into the memories of that time were making the fact that I really had fantasies about her and her raspberry soap in a shower, long before we climbed into that first shower together.

I loved that soap then and now.

"Clear your mind, mister," she said, softly smacking my arm. "We have work to do."

And I tried, I really did. But it's raspberry shampoo, after all.

Chapter 13

Just One Small Problem Named Hank

We got through all of the people we rescued from the ghost slots and found eleven.

We were all convinced there were only the eleven. I'm not a betting man, but I would have bet that was it. Of course, we were betting our entire lives and all the lives in this timeline that we were right.

We were also all exhausted, completely and totally.

"All right, Stan," I said into the air and he appeared.

"Ready for the Bookkeeper's list?" he asked.

"We are," I said.

Lady Luck appeared and sat at the end of the table with Stan. She grabbed one of the cold fries and started biting on it.

I had a master list in front of me and Patty, so I said, "Read off your names."

Lady Luck seemed to have a list as well and was following along.

He did, and I put a check beside each name that agreed with our list.

And then he read the name Hank Carson.

No Hank Carson on our list.

We all looked up at him and he clearly read our expressions.

"Oh, oh," he said.

"Hank's on my list as well," Lady Luck said. "Kronos and I put it together from studying time stream shifts over the last ten years."

I looked at Patty, then at Ben.

"No Hank Carson came out of the machine," I said.

Stan nodded and went on with the list. Everything agreed except that one name.

"How many people are between the two names we agree on?" Stan asked.

"Thirteen," Ben said. "Is Hank Carson a man or a woman?"

"A man," Lady Luck said.

"Then only four men are candidates," he said.

I flipped back through my notes to the four he was talking about and looked at them again.

All five of us did the same. I remembered all four men clearly. All had clearly been from 2004.

After a moment I looked up. "We go back. Look for anything out of place, dig deeper into these four."

Screamer nodded and said, "Ready."

Sherri took Ben's hand, Patty put her hand on my leg.

I took Screamer's hand and Sherri touched his leg.

And once again we were back in front of those damn evil machines.

Concentrate, Ben thought at us.

The first man came out and Screamer pushed him aside. But as he did, Patty slowed down time and we all dove into the poor man's mind.

After what seemed like far too long inside a stranger's head and looking into his very personal thoughts and actions, Screamer thought to us, *He's clean.*

We went on to the next guy.

Same.

And the next guy.

Same.

And the final guy.

Same.

There was no doubt, all four of them were taken by the slots in 2004.

Screamer broke the connection and we all turned to look at Stan and Lady Luck.

"No Hank Carson?" Stan asked.

"No Hank Carson," I said.

"Damn it," Lady Luck said again as she stood. "What the hell is going on here?"

And with that she vanished.

"I hate it when Mom swears," Sherri said, shaking her

head and looking at her notes. "Things tend to turn ugly when that happens."

I could sure understand that. Never wanted to get Lady Luck mad. Something about that just seemed really, really dangerous.

I looked over at Stan. "How many hours do we have left?"

"Ten," he said.

Ten hours to save everyone in the world from being trapped in a nasty time loop. No wonder it was strictly against the rules to time travel. This kind of stuff was just far, far too dangerous.

CHAPTER 14

LOOKING FOR HANK IN ALL THE WRONG PLACES

The moment Lady Luck vanished, Stan got back onto the phone with the Bookkeeper and gave him the name of Hank Carson. "We need every detail about the guy, right down to his shoe size," Stan said.

He listened to the Bookkeeper say something for a moment, nodded and then hung up without saying another word.

"He'll have it all within a half hour," Stan said, sitting back down at the table.

Around us the sky was starting to darken and now the planes coming into the airport had lights on. Pretty soon, stretched out below my invisible floating office, the lights of Las Vegas would be on and in full glory. Normally, I loved looking at those lights from here, but right now I didn't feel much like looking at anything except my hands.

Finally, I took a deep breath, put my hand on Patty's arm, and looked at the group. "So if we didn't pull Hank Carson out of that machine, why are both Kronos and the Bookkeeper showing that he was there and part of what caused this alternate timeline?"

I looked around at my team. "I'm open for theories or even wild speculation."

Screamer shrugged. "He got with one of the survivors and discovered information about the future and used it, thus causing Kronos and the Bookkeeper both to pick up the disruptions he caused."

I nodded. I had figured as much. So if we pulled the others from the past and brought them back to the present, they would never hook up with Hank and thus that would take care of him.

But that was taking a horrible gamble I didn't want to take.

And it honestly didn't feel right to me. My little voice I trusted in poker said that wasn't the right way to go.

"A second option," Sherri said, "is that he's some sort of time traveler that used the trips by the Slots of Saturn to cover his tracks from Kronos."

"There are time travelers?" I asked, feeling stunned.

Sherri nodded. "Mostly from the distant future, but Kronos and his teams keep them out of these times for just this reason."

I glanced at Stan and he was nodding.

"If that's the case, it's out of our hands," I said.

Everyone around the table agreed. If that was the case, that was a problem for Kronos and Laverne.

I looked at everyone. "Any more options, suggestions, or just flat wild theories?"

"The first one seems the most logical," Ben said.

"But that seems like something that Kronos and the Bookkeeper would have taken into account," I said. "All of these people will have talked to some people at one point or another."

"I agree," Screamer said.

"There's something we're missing," I said.

So once again we all sat there in silence.

At that moment, Madge appeared from the diner with a tray of milkshakes. "I can hear all of you thinking clear downstairs," she said, "so thought I would bring some thinking food."

She also had a couple of baskets of hot fries.

I watched as Patty took one, then dropped it and sucked on her thumb.

"Hot out of the fryer," Madge said. "Sorry, should have warned you."

Something just dinged at me really hard.

It was that poker sense of mine that dinged like a little alarm bell to tell me I was missing a detail that was right in front of me.

Patty inspected her thumb for a moment, then put it against the cold glass of the vanilla milkshake in front of us.

Again the little dinger in my head dinged again, like an annoying timer I needed to shut off but couldn't find.

Then it dawned on me what I was seeing.

Patty's thumb.

Hitchhiker.

Someone hadn't been taken inside the slot machines, but had hitchhiked back in time on them.

"Thank you, Madge," I said, sucking on the milkshake so hard it gave me an ice cream headache. "You gave us the answer."

"I did?" she asked, looking puzzled and everyone else looked at me in the same way.

"Patty," I said, "show everyone your burnt thumb."

"It's not really burnt," she said.

"Show them," I said, smiling at her.

She did.

"Now, with your thumb sticking out, make a fist."

She did.

"Of course," Stan said, laughing. "Damn it, Poker Boy, how do you make these weird connections?"

"What connections?" Screamer asked. "Missed me."

Patty was smiling at me and as she did, she stuck out her thumb again over the middle of the table, moving it from left to right as she said, "Going my way, mister?"

"Hitchhiker?" Screamer asked.

Sherri laughed and Ben just nodded.

"We know who we got out of the machine," I said.

"Not who rode on the back of the machine into the past," Stan said.

"Exactly," I said. "I know I never thought of looking around behind those machines."

"I didn't either," Patty said.

"But we have one problem," Stan said. "We don't know exactly when he took that trip back. He wasn't in any of the police reports of those rescued."

"So he went back with one of the first ones," Patty said, "and when the machine jumped again, he got out of the warehouse."

I could feel my stomach tightening up again. Those machines had been operating for almost a week before we got to the warehouse. Hank could have found himself in that warehouse at any point over that week and we wouldn't know when.

Ben looked at me and said, "We have only ten hours to figure out when he arrived there and get him before he gets out of that warehouse. And then get the other eleven back to our time as well."

"If that is how he got back there," Screamer said. "Remember, our first option is the most logical, that he met someone from the future and was influenced by them."

I shook my head. "That doesn't feel right. The Book-keeper would have spotted that. No, I think Hank rode along without meaning to. Not sure why I know that, but just a sense. Now we just have to figure out how."

And with that, again the silence filled the booth and my office overlooking the beautiful city of Las Vegas as the sun slowly set over the western hills.

CHAPTER 15

ONCE MORE INTO THE NIGHTMARE

"So how do we find out when he rode back on the machines?" Sherri asked.

I looked at her and then asked the next logical question. "How could someone ride along and not be in the machine?"

"Touching it from the back," Screamer said.

Beside me, Patty shook her head. "Slot machines in this modern time are almost impossible to get close to from the back, unless he was a maintenance worker or a slot tech. Sitting in one of the other chairs is the most logical thing to have happened."

I couldn't believe I had forgotten that the machine was actually three slot machines.

With three wooden chairs attached.

It was only the machine on the right side that had come

alive and had taken all our focus, but the other two machines rode along because it was a three-machine unit.

"Of course," I said. "We go back again, focus only on the moment the person from this time period was pulled into the machine to see if anyone was sitting next to them."

"And once we spot him," Screamer said, "we'll have a general timeline."

"I agree," Ben said. "We can figure out exactly when the two people on either side from that time were pulled through. That should narrow the time down to a few hours."

"So we go back to the nightmare and inside the heads of the eleven people taken from this time."

Everyone nodded. But clearly none of them were any happier with the idea than I was.

"I'll tell Lady Luck what you are doing," Stan said, and vanished.

Screamer was still sitting in the middle, with Patty on one side and me on the other.

"One more time?" I asked.

"Do we have a choice?" Screamer asked.

"Not that I can think of," I said.

"Then one more time."

Again, we scooted together in the booth and all touched so that our minds were all hooked up.

I thought at everyone, *Focus at the first person from our time and the moment they were at the machine.*

We did just that.

And once again I was back in that warehouse, with the

feeling of panic and fear crawling all over me like a nest of spiders. Sherri instantly calmed all of us down.

Thanks, Patti thought.

Again, with Sherri keeping us calm, I could actually think and get out of the panic I felt back ten years ago as we fought to save over a hundred people from those machines.

We were again in slow motion as Patty had slowed time down, and we were back in our own memories. Then the woman from our time slowly appeared, being spit out by the machine like a bad coin, and Screamer pushed her out of the chair.

Patty slowed the moment down even more so that we could see into the poor woman's mind and see if there happened to be anyone around her that she noticed when she sat at the slots.

No one.

She was the only one in the chairs when the machine took her, and there was no way anyone could get in behind the old slots either, since they were against a wall.

One down, I thought at everyone.

We went through three more people from our time before we found what we were looking for.

The man named Jeffrey Johns, number sixty-four in the list of people we had rescued from the machine. He had just sat down in the chair when the machine was back at Binion's in this time period.

Suddenly, beside him, another man slid into the left seat.

There was a clear thought of annoyance from Jeffrey

because he had been thinking of playing all three slot machines at the same time. Then he was pulled into the machine and into the past.

I got a clear image of the man who sat down in the left chair. Balding head, overweight, Bermuda shorts, and a Hawaiian shirt of loud blues and oranges.

I have a hunch that's him, I thought at everyone.

We check all eleven, Ben thought clearly.

I agreed.

And we did, and that was the only hitchhiker we found from our time back into the past.

Screamer cut the connection and we all moved back into our positions at the booth. Stan had returned and he and Madge were there, waiting for us to return from the nightmare of the past that we had been exploring in our minds.

"We found him," I said, smiling.

Ben quickly looked through his notes. "He arrived in 2004 somewhere in an eight-hour-period of time."

"Great job," Stan said. "Poker Boy, call the Bookkeeper and see if he can narrow the time down some. I'll tell Lady Luck so she can work with Kronos."

Then he vanished.

I grabbed my phone and quickly told the Bookkeeper what we had found and he said simply, "I'll be back with you in twenty minutes."

"So how long did that take?" I asked.

I was known for not wearing a watch or being able to keep

track of time that well. Yet in this countdown, we had to keep track.

"We have just under nine hours to stop the time loop from setting," Ben said.

My heart sank and I could feel what energy I had left sort of draining out of me. And as it did, it was as if I could suddenly hear a huge clock ticking.

Just ticking in the distance.

On and on and on.

Slowly getting louder and taunting me with every tick of the clock.

Chapter 16

Planning The Past

Patty and I sat there sipping our vanilla milkshake. It had partially melted while we were on that last visit back into our shared nightmare, but it was still good. And neither of us cared. We were both just trying to get some energy for whatever came next.

The fries were still just warm enough to eat, so we munched on a few of those as well.

I could tell from Patty's hand on mine that she had been drained by helping Sherri and slowing time even more when we were back in time.

Suddenly, across from us, Sherri, who had been sitting, mostly staring at her milkshake, grabbed her head and bent over in pain.

Screamer instantly had his arm around her and Patty leaned across the table and touched her as well.

I couldn't believe it. The damn slot machines were back again.

I stared at the three of them, wishing I could do something to help.

Stan just sat there staring as well. If a god was helpless, what could I expect to do?

After a moment, Sherri opened her eyes and sat up. Patty leaned back next to me and through the touch in our shoulders I tried to feed her some energy.

"Where are they?" I asked, afraid of the answer.

"A rundown casino out on the old highway," Patty said. "The Golden Jackpot Casino."

"We don't have police on that one," Stan said.

Instantly he and I both jumped to the old casino.

The energy of the evil slot machines pulsed over me like a wave of desire, working to draw me in with the promise of richness and fun, all for a nickel.

An overweight, middle-aged woman, with dyed-brown hair piled far too high for even the 1960s, was headed for the deadly machine. She had on skin-tight green Capri pants that from the back should have had a warning sign attached that told a person to never look. She had a plastic bucket of coins tucked against her left breast and was about five steps from the machine.

Another, even heavier and shorter middle-aged woman dressed in even tighter brown Capri pants was one step behind her.

That was a sight I was never going to get out of my mind,

and if it hadn't been for the pulsing Slots of Saturn machines beyond them, I would have turned away.

Stan and I both jumped again, appearing in front of the women.

We acted like security guards, both holding our hands up for them to stop.

Both women did stop, shocked expressions showing through the layers of makeup coating their faces.

Before they could ask where we came from, Stan said. "These machines are broken." His voice echoed through the casino like only a god can make a voice echo.

"They look fine to me," the first woman said, looking past us both. "I love old slot machines."

"Reminds her of her dearly-departed husband," the other woman said, somehow smiling without cracking the layers of makeup.

"He never had a crank like that one," the first woman said, pointing to the long handle with the black nob on the side of the machine.

Both of them laughed.

I shuddered.

"Yeah, you could wish," the second woman said to her friend, and again they laughed.

Behind me I could feel the intense pull of the machines, demanding that someone sit down and feed them.

In front of me were two women who really did belong in the past, but a past far before 2004.

"What can one pull hurt?" the first woman asked, giving

Stan a smile that I swore should have broken a couple of layers of caked-on makeup. Her teeth were yellow from too many cigarettes.

"More than you know," Stan said.

He waved his hands at the two women and they vanished.

"Where did you send them?" I asked, looking around to make sure no one had gotten in behind us.

"To the buffet, paid lunch," he said.

"Yeah, that's what they needed," I said, shaking my head.

We spread out a little and for the next three minutes we stood there, backs to the machines, telling people the slots were damaged, as the power of the slots drew people toward them.

Finally, the machines started pulsing bright to dim and then back, more and more, faster and faster, until finally with a flash they jumped back to the warehouse in the past.

They had left empty.

Around us the old casino went on, an occasional bell going off, an occasional yell from a drunk at one of the gaming tables. Without the pulsing energy of the old slot machines, the casino suddenly felt worn and tired. And it smelled of old cigarettes and spilled whiskey on the worn blue carpet.

"Lucky we had Sherri to tell us the slots were here again," I said.

He nodded. "But while you are in the past, she needs to stay here to keep watch."

"I agree," I said.

We both jumped back to my office where Sherri looked like she was just recovering from the jolt of the machine's last jump.

And Patty looked even more tired than before.

I just hoped that at some point this would be over and Patty could rest.

Not that I worried about her or anything.

Chapter 17

The Plan

We knew that the other eleven people from the future all came back out of the slot machine in just over an hour period as we rescued everyone. We knew that time exactly.

And we knew who they were and what they looked like, so we could intercept them on the way out of the warehouse to the police that we had stationed outside that first time.

But Hank had arrived in a window that the Bookkeeper could only knock down to four hours.

Four hours to find him and get him back, a couple hours to get everyone else back.

Six hours.

We had eight hours until the time loop locked in and trapped us forever. And not even Kronos, the God of Time, could save us.

That was cutting it very close.

Too close for my tastes.

Laverne appeared and nodded to Stan, then to her daughter, then to me as she sat down. She was now dressed in casual clothes. Jeans and a tan sweatshirt that said, "Believe It" on the front.

"Great job stopping yet another one," she said.

"Sherri knew where it came in," I said. "Stan and I just stood guard."

Laverne nodded. "Good team work. So, who is going back with me to stop this madness?"

I looked around at my team and sighed. I had given this a little thought and I knew I was right. But both Patty and Screamer were not going to like it.

"I think you and Ben and I should go back," I said to Laverne. It felt weird giving Lady Luck instructions, but she had asked after all.

One of her dark eyebrows actually went up at that suggestion, telling me it wasn't what she expected.

Both Screamer and Patty started to object and I held up my hand and they stopped.

"We need to keep Sherri here in case the machines come back. Screamer, you and Patty need to be here to help her through that. In the time we're gone, the slots might come back more than once."

Sherri didn't like the sound of that, but she nodded.

I turned to my boss. "Stan, you need to be here to jump to

stop anyone else from getting sent back if the machines do come back again."

Stan nodded.

"That's critical," Laverne said, "because we don't have time to figure all this again."

Screamer nodded and so did Sherri.

I looked at Ben and he smiled.

"Ben knows exactly what each person looks like," I said, "so we're not trusting my memory completely. And he knows which casino they came from in this time, and when, so they can be transported to that same spot close to the time they left. That way they will never be reported missing."

Lady Luck smiled, but Patty didn't look happy.

"I'll work with my friend Johnny in the past," I said. "He was the local cop friend that helped us. He can help me pull out the right ones and keep them from going outside to the police. We'll jump them out from back in the shadows of the warehouse."

And then I looked at Lady Luck. "And you get to do all the transporting through time to where Ben says they need to go."

"A sound plan," Laverne said. "We need to get going, we're cutting this a little close."

I turned to Patty and kissed her.

She kissed me back, then said, "Make this work."

"I'll do my best," I said, smiling at her. Then as I pulled away I said, "Just have the raspberry soap ready to go."

"Oh, damn you two," Screamer said.

Sherri blushed and Patty blushed and Ben just shook his head.

It made me smile.

A moment later, Lady Luck transported me and Ben and herself ten years into the past and into the middle of a dark warehouse full of old and creepy slot machines stacked in rows that seemed to go on forever.

All of them dead, looking very much like tombstones in a graveyard in the dim light.

To one side of the warehouse was a very dangerous set of slots pulsing, sending off a light that made the big warehouse seem even more daunting and huge.

And then with a bright flash, the warehouse went completely dark.

"They jumped," I said.

"And as soon as they come back," Ben said in the dark, "we'll know if we are in the right time window."

"I hope so," Lady Luck said, her voice beside me in the dark. "We have very little margin of error."

CHAPTER 18

FINDING HANK

While the machines were gone I teleported to the front of the warehouse where I remembered a light switch being, and flipped it on.

Overhead lights clicked on, showing the gigantic size of this slot graveyard. It had to be at least two football fields long and another one wide, and the slots were stacked on shelves a good twenty feet over my head in long rows from front to back.

Laverne and Ben joined me and we went over to one side at the head of the aisle where the slots were. I pointed to a tarp that still seemed to be covering something, only if you looked hard, there was nothing there. The tarp just seemed to be floating in space. Some part of the machine never left the warehouse when it jumped.

"My gut sense is that riding on the outside of this thing

isn't going to be a pleasant experience," I said. "Hank will appear under that tarp, more than likely knocked out cold."

Both Laverne and Ben nodded.

"I'm going to check the other doors to make sure none of them are unlocked or broken open from the inside," I said. "I know he didn't go out the front door because it had a padlock on it when we arrived the first time."

"Good thinking," Ben said.

I teleported to the back of the warehouse and checked the door on the right. Secure. I jumped to the garage door and it was also secure.

Suddenly I heard Laverne in my head, *They are returning.*

I jumped back to where they were just as the machine appeared under the tarp.

There was no one in the chair under the tarp.

Damn.

The machines sat there, covered, their glow taunting me, pulling me to go sit down at them.

"Wow, that's some pull," Ben said.

"They are very powerful," Laverne said.

"I'm going to check the other door," I said.

I jumped and the instant I saw the door, I knew we were in trouble. It had been broken out from the inside.

Hank had already gotten out into the world.

I jumped back to Laverne and Ben. "He's been here," I said.

"Damn," Lady Luck said. "When was the previous jump that we know about?"

"Six hours ago," Ben said.

Laverne nodded and looked up. "Kronos, help?"

Suddenly we were back in a dark warehouse, and again through the darkness, the machine was pulsing, getting ready to jump.

"Check the door," Laverne said a moment before I vanished to do just that.

It was locked and hadn't been broken out.

"Thank the heavens," I said.

I flipped on the lights from near the back door and was about to jump back to Laverne and Ben when suddenly Hank appeared out of nowhere and hit me on the side of the head.

I had a fraction of an instant of warning from one of my superpower senses, but they were tuned to slower warnings like what I needed at a poker table.

Not someone about to hit me.

But still I managed to move just enough to cause Hank's intended blow with an old slot handle to just graze my head.

I went down hard, but somehow stayed alert enough to say, "Hank's here!"

And then I took myself out of time, freezing Hank as he was about to smash open the back door of the warehouse.

Ben and Laverne appeared above me in the time bubble.

Ben reached down and helped me to my feet.

"You all right?" Laverne asked, frowning and looking at the side of my head like a worried mom.

I could feel I was bleeding slightly from a gash on the side of my head, and I knew for a fact I was going to have a nasty headache, but I wasn't about to tell Lady Luck herself that I wasn't all right.

"I'll be fine," I said. "My Spidey sense warned me just in time."

Ben laughed.

Laverne just looked puzzled.

"I'm going to take him back," Laverne said, nodding at Hank.

She waved a hand at him and he went to the ground like a sack of very rotten Idaho potatoes.

"Wow, nifty power," I said. "Can I learn that one?"

She laughed. "Hang around for a few more centuries and I might teach it to you. I'll tell everyone at the office we got Hank and then be back."

Then she and Hank were gone.

Ben handed me a wad of Kleenex from his pocket for the bleeding and I nodded thanks. I pressed it against the side of my head as we started walking silently up the aisle between shelves and shelves of old slot machines, a reminder of many people's dead dreams.

CHAPTER 19

JOHNNY DOES A DOUBLE TAKE

Laverne appeared as we neared the front.

"They stopped another attack," she said. "And they were happy we got Hank."

I nodded. Damn I missed Patty, even being away from her for this long seemed wrong these days. We were a team. I was stronger and smarter and much calmer with her around.

"I'm going to jump us to about a half hour before you guys start bringing people out," Laverne said.

"Too close," I said. "It took us a while to figure it out. Make it forty-five minutes."

She nodded and the next thing I knew we were standing off on the other side of the warehouse, away from the Slots of Saturn.

Something really bothered me and I looked around. Then as I heard the doorknob rattle, I knew the problem.

97

"Lights."

I teleported to right in front of the front door, clicked off the lights, and jumped back to a spot beside Laverne.

A moment later I heard my own voice and the lights came back on.

"Quick thinking," Ben whispered.

We stood there for the next half hour, listening to the echoes of our talk, letting me relive once again one of the most horrid times of my life. But now from what seemed like the grandstands.

If I didn't already have a headache from the hit across the head, this time-travel stuff would give me one.

Then, finally, my younger self and Patty and Screamer started rescuing people from the machine.

"Here we go," I whispered. "Ben, you watch and when you see the first one, you tell Laverne."

He nodded.

"Do you need to be touching the person to jump them back to our time?"

"No," Lady Luck said. "Ben just tell me when and where as exact as you can."

"I will," he said.

We stood in the shadows, watching as Johnny and Geneva helped the rescues from the Slots of Saturn out into the hot air and the waiting arms of ambulances and police.

"The first one," Ben said, nodding as Johnny brought her around the corner from the machines and started toward the front door, helping her along as he went.

He then told Lady Luck exactly when, right to the minute, and which casino the woman had come from and what area.

Laverne nodded. "Be right back."

The woman disappeared right out of Johnny's arms.

I stepped forward and motioned for Johnny to come into the shadows with me.

"Poker Boy?" he asked, looking very puzzled and looking back over his shoulder at the same time.

"It's me," I said.

"Geneva says you are still back there getting another person out."

"I am," I said. "That me, from this time. I'm from ten years in the future."

He started to open his mouth and I waved my hand. "We have some people the machine took from my time ten years in the future. We will just be taking those people out of your hands and getting them back to where they belong. But you and Geneva keep this to yourselves. Don't ever tell the other me, or anyone for that matter. Okay?"

He nodded, still looking puzzled and hesitant.

"Go back to work," I said. "It is critical you and the team over there get the people out of that machine."

He nodded and turned away.

I teleported back into the shadows in another aisle so when he looked back, I would have vanished.

Laverne appeared and nodded she had been successful. But she was looking a little tired.

And that bothered me a lot.

I glanced at Ben and he was looking at her as well, looking worried.

Lady Luck should never look tired.

Ever.

CHAPTER 20

A CHANGE OF PLANS

After the next two jumps for Laverne back to the present, she looked horrible.

When she came back after the second one, she actually staggered some.

I looked at Ben and he looked very concerned.

I needed to do something and do it fast.

"Change of plans," I said as we waited for the next one from the future. "We have eight more and we're going to hold them all here and all of us jump as a group back to my office. Can you do that?" I asked Laverne. "Just one more jump?"

"I think so," she said, her voice weak. "Kronos warned me this might not be possible. Time jumping takes a massive amount of energy. More than I had imagined, actually. More than I have ever spent in thousands and thousands of years."

That was not something I wanted to hear.

"Just sit there against those slots in the shadows and rest," I said. "Ben and I will get the other eight people rounded up."

She nodded and slid down to the ground. "Thanks."

I looked at Ben and he nodded and we went back to watching the people being rescued from the machine. In all my years, I would never have imagined giving Lady Luck orders, let alone seeing one of the most powerful gods in all the universe exhausted.

Now I just hoped she had enough energy to get us all back at once to my office. From there, Stan could take care of getting the survivors to the right places and times. Otherwise, all of us were going to be stuck in a very ugly time loop that ended with Patty and me ten years apart.

I didn't even want to think about that.

"Next one," Ben said.

The woman was being escorted by Johnny.

I stepped out into the light and walked up to Johnny, who again looked surprised to see me.

"That's one of them," I said. "We need her to wait in here with us."

Johnny nodded and I led the way into a side aisle. I quickly pulled a few tarps off of slots and put them on the concrete. "Just sit there and rest," I said to the woman. "We'll have you home shortly."

"Another one," Ben said as Geneva escorted another man from our time toward the front door.

I moved out as Johnny headed back toward the machines

and motioned for Geneva to bring the man over and I had him sit on the tarp as well.

"What's going on?" he demanded.

"We're trying to get you home," I said.

He started to stand and I froze him, pulling myself and Ben out of time.

"We need help," I whispered to Ben.

He nodded. "Who can we trust?"

I knew at once who to call.

"Stan," I said, "A little help?"

Ben shook his head. "Stan can't jump through time."

"I can't what?" Stan asked, then looked at me and Ben.

"Oh," Ben said.

I had called the Stan of this time, not the future Stan.

"That you, Ben?" Stan asked, smiling. "What are you doing here? It's been a long time."

"Working on Poker Boy's team from ten years in the future," Ben said.

Stan started to open his mouth and I stopped him. "We can't tell you anything and you can't say a word that you saw us here."

"What's happening?"

"We're trying to rescue people the machine took from ten years in the future," I said.

His face went white as he instantly understood some of the problem.

"We need help with holding these people in place until the

last ones get out of the machine and we can jump them all back to the future."

He nodded.

"Can you help us and never say a word, not even to Laverne."

"Does she know you are here?" he asked.

"I do," Laverne said, staggering around the corner and again sitting down, her back against a slot machine. "But I'm blocking my past self or any other gods from seeing any of this."

Stan nodded. "Not a word. What can I do?"

"Hold these people while Poker Boy and Ben round up the rest," Laverne said. "Then give me an energy boost when I try to jump us all back to our time."

"I can do that," he said, nodding.

I dropped the time bubble and Ben turned back to the steady stream of people again starting from the machines toward the front door.

Behind me the two people from the future were sitting on the floor, frozen, not moving.

Another power I really needed to learn at some point.

CHAPTER 21

TOO CLOSE—FAR, FAR TOO CLOSE

After we had the seventh person sitting frozen on the tarp, I looked at Ben. "How much time do we have?"

"Thirty-seven minutes," he said. "The last one from the future should be out in fifteen minutes."

"Well," I said, "that's going to be a long fifteen minutes."

He only nodded.

"And this is cutting it far, far too close."

Again he nodded.

"Too close?" Stan asked.

"You'll know in ten years. If this works."

I looked at Lady Luck. She was still sitting on the floor with her eyes closed. But at least now she had some color in her cheeks again, as much as I could see color in the gray shadows of the thousands of dead slot machines towering around us.

Stan just kept staring at me, shaking his head.

"Sorry, can't tell you anything," I said, smiling at him. "You know that."

He laughed. "Hell, this is going to be a tough enough secret to hold for ten years."

"Well, keep it," I said, "and we'll all owe you big time."

"That we will," Lady Luck said, without opening her eyes.

After that, we stood there, watching each and every person rescued from the Slots of Saturn be helped to the front door of the warehouse and out into the heat of the day.

I forced myself to relax as much as possible. I had a hunch that Ben and I both were going to have to help Laverne make this jump to the future. I wasn't sure how, but I bet it would include feeding her energy. Last thing we would need would be to get stuck five years from now.

Finally, after what seemed like an eternity as time had slowed down and slowed down, Ben said, "That's him."

I also recognized the guy being escorted by Johnny.

I moved out into the light and took the dazed man's arm, then looked at Johnny. "This is the last one. Remember, not a word."

"You got it."

"Thanks," I said.

"I expect when the timelines catch up, you find me with a full explanation."

"I promise," I said.

I took the man over into the shadows where Laverne was now standing.

"Gather everyone together tightly," she said.

Her voice still didn't sound strong, but it sounded better than it had a little bit ago.

Stan and I and Ben did what she asked, with the eight people from the slot all in some sort of trance. I have no idea how Stan did that, but I sure wanted to know.

I'd ask him if this worked and we got back.

"Push them tight together," Laverne said. "The three of us need to be holding hands around them.

Stan helped us arrange that until I was pushed in tight against a middle-aged woman wearing far too much perfume. I just hoped I didn't sneeze in the middle of all this.

I had a hold of Laverne's hand on one side and Ben's on the other.

"Stan, stay about five feet away," Laverne said, "but focus as much energy at me as you can right now."

I could feel the energy pouring from Stan into Laverne as Stan stepped back and leaned forward and focused at Laverne.

Then, after a few moments of soaking in energy from Stan, Laverne said, "Ben, Poker Boy, on the count of three, focus every bit of energy you both have through your hands to me."

"Understood," I said, taking a deep breath.

"Understood," Ben said.

"Kronos," Lady Luck said into the air. "A little help would be appreciated right about now."

Then with Stan still focusing energy at her, Lady Luck said, "One. Two. Three. Go!"

Every ounce of energy I had I imagined it pouring through my fingers and into Lady Luck. I knew how to do that since Patty and I did that all the time with each other, but not at this level.

I felt like I was turning myself inside out.

This was life or death.

There was no point in holding back any ounce of energy if I ever wanted to see Patty again.

And that thought made me pour out even more energy to Lady Luck.

Around us the warehouse vanished.

And then nothing for the longest time, or what seemed to be the longest time.

I just kept pushing energy at Laverne with all my focus.

Suddenly, we were in my office floating over the city of Las Vegas, in front of the big booth.

The eight survivors and Laverne and Ben and I all tumbled to the ground in a bad imitation of a mass Twister Game gone horribly wrong.

The woman with too much perfume smashed me into the floor.

The only thing I remember seeing was Patty's wonderful face, panicked as she jumped out of the booth to come and help.

Then the room went black as I think I passed out.

CHAPTER 22

THE MAGIC TOUCH

I wasn't sure how long it was, but the next thing I remember was Patty stroking my forehead lightly. I could feel a little energy from her touch reviving me a little.

Every bone in my body ached.

And my head hurt from where Hank had hit me with that slot machine handle.

And I wanted to sneeze something awful.

I opened my eyes and smiled at the love of my life, who was smiling at me with those huge brown eyes of hers.

"You all right?"

"No idea," I said, honestly.

She helped me sit up.

I was still on the floor in front of the booth and Madge was hurrying in with three glasses of water.

Sherri and Screamer were sitting next to Laverne on the floor and Stan was helping Ben to sit up.

"What happened to all the people?" I managed to ask with a hoarse throat.

Patty handed me a glass of water that tasted wonderful and gave me even more energy.

"Kronos brought Burt and some of the other gods and got them all back to their right places and times," Stan said.

Laverne nodded. Then she looked at Stan with a look that I hoped someday to have her look at me with. "Thank you."

"Yes, thank you," I said, smiling at my boss.

He smiled. "It was worse in the last five hours knowing what I knew from that side, but not knowing how we got there, or if it would even work. Kronos says it did. We're back in the main timeline. Everything is reset."

Patty hugged me, smiling, and I could feel even more energy pouring through me.

"Mom," Sherri said, "Let me get you home and into bed."

Lady Luck nodded, but didn't move. "Stan, want to jump us both there and come back. Not sure if I dare risk it yet."

Stan nodded and the three of them vanished.

Patty was working to get me to my feet and into the booth and Screamer was helping Ben up from the floor when Stan appeared.

"Stan, same kind of help if you don't mind?" Ben asked.

Stan nodded and smiled. He looked at me. "We have some talking to do."

"Tomorrow," I said.

He laughed. "Tomorrow. Great work, once again."

He vanished with Ben.

"You two going to be all right?" Screamer asked.

I nodded. "After some rest."

"Great work," he said, "as always."

"You too," I said. "Tell Madge we're done for the night."

He nodded and turned and went through the door into Madge's Diner.

Outside the windows of my office, I could see the hint of sunrise starting to color the eastern hills. Below, the lights of Vegas looked wonderful.

It felt great to be home.

I couldn't remember being so tired.

And so satisfied at the same time. Especially sitting there in the booth of my office, holding Patty.

Finally, she pushed away from me and waved her hand. "You need a shower, big boy."

"Sweat?" I asked, smiling at her.

"Perfume," she said.

I stood and she held me as we headed for the door to her apartment below.

"You might need to soap me up some," I said, smiling at her. "I'm pretty tired."

"Raspberry soap?" she asked, smiling back and hugging me.

"Of course," I said. "Just like the first time ten years ago."

"I don't think either one of us has the energy to do what we did that first time ten years ago," she said, kissing me as we went through the door and into her wonderful apartment.

And, of course, she was right.

But the next night we certainly tried to repeat what we had done ten years before in that wonderful shower with that wonderful-smelling soap.

And we honestly came pretty darned close.

And in sex and raspberry soap showers, pretty darned close is pretty darned nice.

The Fun STARTS HERE

Just Turn The Page...

SNEAK PEEK

BEING DEAD (THE FIRST YEAR)

CHAPTER ONE

Dying on a first date sucks.

Dying on a blind date sucks even worse.

Especially when your date dies with you. And then goes off through some tunnel of light into the next life or something, leaving you sitting alone, dead, in a dark alley, waiting for your own tunnel of light.

Hands down, the worst ending to any date in recorded history.

The alley we had been forced to go into was blacker than the inside of a latrine, and seeing how it smelled, I would have not been surprised to be in a latrine, but I knew I wasn't since it seemed that being dead meant I could see just fine in the dark.

And smell just fine as well. Holy crap. The nearby Chinese restaurant garbage smelled like my fridge after six days of feeling sorry for myself and laying on the couch and eating take-out without taking out the uneaten food in the original cartons. And no telling how many homeless and drunks had actually used this alley for a bathroom.

I was sitting on a big green dumpster owned by a nearby office, so thankfully it didn't have the odor of the other dumpsters coming up between my legs.

The scum with the greasy black hair and dirty ski parka that had killed us was going through my date's pockets as I sat and watched.

The guy looked skinny and no doubt drug-addicted. His motions were jerky, his eyes darting around him like a rat trying to find a way out of a maze.

My blind date, dear old Handsome Bob, as I had started to think of him for the full thirty minutes I had known him, had caused this mess by thinking he could be a macho asshole or something.

The scum with the greasy black hair had approached us on the sidewalk and Bob had shaken his head and said, "Not now."

We were headed down the street to a nice Italian restaurant that served the best red wine and bread plate this side of New York. And that was going some for the Old Towne section of Boise, Idaho.

Bob was dressed in a clearly expensive silk suit and no tie, while I didn't look so cheap myself. For the date I had put on dark slacks, a white silk blouse with pearls around my neck, and a thin see-through sweater. No bra because I wanted my date to get an occasional peek at what might be offered after dinner if things went right.

Sitting dead in an alley sure wasn't my idea of things going right.

The greasy jerk had pulled out a gun, his hands shaking. Dear old dead Handsome Bob had said, "You don't want to do that."

Bless him.

Clearly the druggie did want to do exactly what he was doing, but I didn't say that. I was busy ramping up one of my super powers.

You see, before I was so suddenly cut down, I had worked as a superhero in the housing and hotel industry. Over the last century I had worked both front desks of hotels and sold real estate. At the moment I was on the real estate side, trying to help out in the booming Boise real estate market.

Amazing the kind of crap that goes on in real estate when big money is involved.

I hit greasy-hair with a full dose of my calming power. The guy was so high on drugs my power actually didn't do anything but make him stop shaking so hard.

He pointed to the dark alley with the gun. "Get in there and then dig out your money."

"And if we say no?" Handsome Bob asked the guy.

Since Bob was almost a foot taller than the greasy-haired druggie, I suppose Bob thought he could bully the situation a little.

Bless dear old now-dead stupid Bob.

I hit the guy with another dose of calming power. I had enough power on a normal day to stop a shouting, irate, pissed-off hotel customer at a front desk and make them smile.

The guy with the gun got calmer, but his pea brain was still set on robbing us. At least I got him to not shoot us right there on the sidewalk because of Handsome Bob's stupidity.

"Let's just give him our stuff and he will let us go," I said to Bob.

"Smart woman," the guy said, smiling and showing a mouthful of rotted teeth.

Actually, I had planned that when we got into the alley I would simply jump us away from this nut and then figure out something to tell dear old Bob.

Bob didn't know I was a one-hundred-year-old superhero and could just teleport anywhere I wanted. Not something you tell someone before a first blind date. Men tended to have sexual problems when they realized the woman they were with was over a hundred.

Bob nodded to me and we walked the twenty steps into the alley, Bob pushing me slightly ahead of him.

Then, as we stopped and turned at just about the point where the rotted Chinese food odor got the worst, Bob went to lunge at the guy.

Handsome Bob went to really, really stupid Bob very quickly.

I was so surprised Bob would do something that idiotic, I didn't react fast enough to jump us out of there.

The guy fired, hitting Bob in the arm.

The bullet went through Bob's flesh and hit me square between the eyes.

Now that was a shocker, let me tell you.

One moment I am standing alive in the alley and the next I am a ghost sitting on a smelly dumpster watching dear old Handsome Bob hold his arm and swear.

The greasy-haired guy was now twitching again. He stared at my body lying there in the alley, clearly getting my wonderful blouse and sweater all stained up with my own blood.

Then he looked at Bob, who was also staring at me, holding his wounded arm and looking sick to his stomach.

Then the guy did what any self-respecting murderer would do. He shot Bob.

Bob slumped to the ground and the guy fired one more shot into Bob's head.

A moment later I watched Bob's ghost stand up, look around, then look up and float off into a white light.

"Nice meeting you jerk-face," I shouted after Bob.

I was pretty sure he didn't hear me.

As I said, the worst ending to a blind date ever.

CHAPTER TWO

The druggie who had killed me and my blind date started through Bob's pockets. The druggie pulled out a money clip and then took Bob's watch. Then he rolled Bob over slightly and took out his wallet.

He pulled out a single-package condom and tossed it aside.

I just shook my head. "Damn, Bob, only one? Where was the confidence? If you had come back to my place, you would have needed at least three just to make it to breakfast."

The greasy murderer clearly didn't hear me. And I had a hunch dead Bob didn't either.

I glanced around. I was still the only ghost in the alley.

Where was my greeting party?

I figured I had become a Ghost Agent, which was why I hadn't gotten the beam-of-light ride. I had never met a Ghost

Agent, but I had heard from my best friend Patty that she and her boyfriend, Poker Boy, had worked with some Ghost Agents just lately to save the world. Seems Patty and her boyfriend were always saving the world, which I must admit I appreciated.

The guy stood and stepped toward my body.

"Hey, not so fast there, jerk-face," I said, jumping down from the dumpster and brushing off my pants.

The greasy-haired slime-ball picked up my clutch purse and went through it. That I didn't much care about. I had a few hundred in there and that was that.

But then he looked around at the mouth of the alley and then looked back at me with that look I had seen scum like him get. Ghost or no ghost, he wasn't touching me, even if I did have a hole in the middle of my forehead.

This night had gone bad enough as it was.

The guy kneeled down beside my body and I took two quick steps at the guy and went to kick him clear across the alley.

Foot went right through him. Charlie Brown would have been proud of my form, though. I didn't end up on my back.

However, when my foot went through the guy, I got to read all of his thoughts.

All of what he was about to do to me.

So I closed my eyes and went inside the scum. Now I knew for a fact I was in a cesspool, swimming in the shit that this guy called thoughts. If I got out of here I would need about ten showers.

If ghosts took showers.

As he reached for my right breast, I shouted at the top of my lungs, "No!"

And trust me, I can be loud.

Just ask anyone who sat beside me at a Broncos' football game.

And I was inside the guy when I shouted.

Slime-bucket grabbed his head and rolled over backward, the intense pain striking everywhere.

As he rolled away, I managed to stand my ground and get out of his body. I shook myself, wishing I could forget the memories of what I had just seen in his mind.

It would take twenty showers before I would feel clean again.

The guy was holding his head and screaming and rolling on the ground. Blood was coming out of his ears.

Both ears.

"Wow, what did you do to him?" a voice behind me asked.

I turned around to see a handsome couple standing to one side looking shocked. Both were about my height of five-ten, both wore jeans, expensive shirts, and tennis shoes.

"The pervert was about to get his jollies on my dead body, so I climbed inside his head and shouted as loud as I could."

Both of them laughed.

Then the woman stepped forward. "I'm Jewel and this is Tommy. We came to help get you used to being a ghost, but guess you are doing just fine."

I shook both their hands, happy as hell I had company.

"I'm Marble Grant. And got a hunch I'm going to need a lot of help."

"Someone close to you?" Tommy asked, pointing at Handsome Bob.

"Knew him for thirty minutes," I said. "Blind date. But I had planned on getting much closer to him after dinner, if you get my drift."

Jewel laughed and Tommy actually blushed a little, which I loved. I had a feeling I was going to like these two.

"I suppose you two are Ghost Agents. Right?"

Both of them looked shocked.

"I was a superhero in the hospitality and real estate side of the world," I said. "Any chance you two know Patty Ledgerwood and Poker Boy?"

"We do," Jewel said.

"You know," I said, "I'm damn hungry and I assume there is a way ghosts eat, so any chance we could get out of this smell and grab a bite and you guys call Patty and have her meet us. I would kind of like to tell her about my sudden death myself, since she has been my best friend for a hundred years now, give or take."

Both of them just nodded.

"Anything we need to do with that guy?" I asked, looking down at the scum who had killed me and Handsome Bob before I had the chance to find out if the handsome part went all the way to Bob's southern regions.

Greasy hair was still rolling on the dirty concrete, holding his ears and screaming. He was losing a lot of blood through his fingers. I clearly had done some damage.

"I think he's finished," Tommy said, laughing.

"Yeah," Jewel said. "Got to remember that trick."

With that we jumped to a place I knew well and loved, the Golden Nugget Buffet in downtown Las Vegas.

Now I knew I was really going to like these two.

Chapter Three

The Golden Nugget Buffet had been decorated in all warm brown cloth and polished brass. Plants ringed the outside of the side part of the dining room nearest the escalator and the tables were solid, as were the chairs.

My hand went right through a chair as I tried to pull it out and Jewel did it for me.

"You'll learn how to actually move some physical matter, but you don't want to do that too often because people start to get spooked."

"I'll bet," I said.

Tommy jumped away to find Patty, and Jewel led me up to the wonderful smelling food. The images from the murderer's head were slowly fading, something I was very grateful for.

"Be careful to not run into anyone," Jewel said, indicating the six people around the large buffet area. "You end up reading their thoughts."

"Yeah, learned that with the guy who shot me," I said.

Jewel showed me how to pick up a plate, which was actually just the ghost component of the plate, and how to take food from the buffet.

In five minutes of filling a ghost plate with ghost food, I managed to not run into anyone alive, which sort of felt like a victory. I called it the dance of the living. A living person came toward me, I stepped sideways and went around them.

Jewel did the same, seemingly without noticing.

Back at the table, I bit into a piece of prime rib and damn near had an orgasm right there at the table.

Jewel just smiled as I moaned and kept on eating the fantastic tasting food.

"I remember the food being good here," I said after a few bites, "but never this good."

"Everything is better when you are a ghost," Jewel said. "Food tastes better, emotions are more powerful, and the travel and living is easier."

"Sex?" I asked.

"As the joke goes," Jewel said, smiling, "it's to die for."

"Oh, no," I said. "I had enough trouble controlling myself when I was alive."

Jewel just laughed and at that moment Tommy appeared.

"Patty is in Poker Boy's office," Tommy said. "Let's just

grab some food and jump there. She's expecting us but doesn't know why yet."

It dawned on me why Patty couldn't jump here. She was still alive. Anyone in the restaurant would see her arrive and then talk to no one. Not a good idea.

Tommy headed for the buffet. I really needed to pee, but instead I kept eating as we waited for him. Damn, the food was so good. I was going to be lucky to not gain a ton of weight now that I had died. I needed to remember to ask Jewel and Tommy how they stayed so thin.

After Tommy came back with a full plate of food, he jumped the three of us and our food and drink to what I assumed was Poker Boy's office, although I had never been there.

In fact, the place was like a legend.

But I had heard it was something special and I had heard right. The office wasn't really an office. It was more like a tile platform floating in the air a thousand feet over the Strip.

All four walls were freaking clear glass with a wood railing about waist high all the way around.

Without that railing, I would have been so afraid of falling off that slick checkered tile floor, I would have been clinging to the furniture and screaming like a ten-year-old girl not wanting to go see her uncle.

And I was dead, so pretty certain the fall wouldn't kill me again.

Still, scary damn place and now I really had to pee.

I made my heart stop racing and looked around.

In the very center of the room was this huge 1950s style diner booth, with a scarred tabletop and red vinyl booth seats on three sides. The thing was big enough to hold ten people if the people really liked each other.

There were half-a-dozen chairs around the room that could be pulled up to the open end of the booth I suppose, but three of them just sat facing out over the incredible view of the city.

And wow, what a view. I had always loved the lights of Las Vegas. Just never seen them from the air like this before.

"Marble," Patty said as we appeared. "Tommy said you needed to talk with me. Everything all right? You could have just called you know?"

"Not sure I knew how exactly," I said, smiling at my best friend.

Jewel laughed as she set her food and mine on the booth table.

Patty was wearing her MGM Grand Front Desk uniform of dark slacks, tan blouse and a lighter tan vest. She had her long hair pulled back and was as stunning as ever.

Patty frowned, something I had rarely seen her do in a century.

I glanced at my food on the booth table, then turned back to my friend. "Got myself killed while on a blind date about thirty minutes ago."

Patty's eyes went totally round. "Are you all right?"

"Pretty sure I'm dead," I said, laughing. I pointed to my forehead. "Bullet right there did the trick."

Patty looked like she was about to cry.

"Can I hug her?" I asked, glancing back at Jewel.

"She's a superhero," Jewel said, "and she can see you, so sure, don't know why not?"

I stepped toward Patty and she hugged me so hard, I wasn't sure I would be able to breathe.

And I hugged her back.

I guess, for the first time, it was sinking in that I had really died.

I was still here but I was dead.

That just sucked.

Except for the part about the food tasting so much better.

Finish Reading

Being Dead (The First Year): A Marble Grant Novel

Get More Marble Grant

DeanWesleySmithStore.com

Hear From Dean

Want More From Dean?

For Dean Wesley Smith's newsletter
go to deanwesleysmith.com.

Get the latest news and releases from all of WMG's authors
and lines, including Kristine Grayson, Kris Nelscott,
Pulphouse Magazine, and so much more...

To sign up, **go to wmgbooks.com.**

About the Author
DEAN WESLEY SMITH

Considered one of the most prolific writers working in modern fiction, *New York Times* and *USA Today* bestselling writer, Dean Wesley Smith published over two hundred novels and over seven hundred books in forty years, and hundreds and hundreds of short stories. He has over thirty million copies of his books in print.

At the moment he produces novels in four major series, including the time travel **Thunder Mountain** novels set in the old west, the galaxy-spanning **Seeders Universe** series, the cold case mystery series, **Cold Poker Gang** series, and the superhero series staring **Poker Boy.**

During his career, Dean also wrote a couple dozen *Star Trek* novels, the only two original *Men in Black* novels, Spider-Man and X-Men novels, plus novels set in gaming and television worlds. Writing with his wife Kristine Kathryn Rusch under the name Kathryn Wesley, they wrote the novel for the NBC miniseries **The Tenth Kingdom** and other books for *Hallmark Hall of Fame* movies.

He wrote novels under dozens of pen names in the worlds

of comic books and movies, including novelizations of almost a dozen films, from *X-Men* to *The Final Fantasy* to *Steel* to *Rundown*.

Dean also worked as a fiction editor off and on, starting at Pulphouse Publishing, then at *VB Tech Journal*, then Pocket Books, and now at WMG Publishing where he and Kristine Kathryn Rusch serve as executive editors for the acclaimed *Fiction River* anthology series. He took over the editorship of the acclaimed *Pulphouse Magazine* in 2018.

For more information about Dean's books and ongoing projects, please visit his website at www.deanwesleysmith.com

facebook.com/deanwsmith3

patreon.com/deanwesleysmith

bookbub.com/authors/dean-wesley-smith